# RAINBOW STEW

by

## Cathryn Falwell

Lee & Low Books Inc. *New York*

A special thanks for Louise's patience, Eamae's perspective, Alex's
support, Peter's encouragement, and the cheers from my gardening
and cooking friends.

LEE & LOW BOOKS Inc., 95 Madison Avenue, New York, NY 10016
leeandlow.com
Manufactured in China by Toppan, February 2013
Book design by David and Susan Neuhaus/NeuStudio
Book production by The Kids at Our House
The text is set in 26-point Dannette and 17-point Wilke
The illustrations are rendered in multimedia collage

10 9 8 7 6 5 4 3 2 1
First Edition

Library of Congress Cataloging-in-Publication Data
Falwell, Cathryn.
Rainbow Stew / by Cathryn Falwell. — First edition.
        pages cm
    Summary: "On a rainy summer day, three children and their grandpa pick vegetables in his garden
and then cook and share a delicious meal of his famous Rainbow Stew. Includes recipe"— Provided
by publisher.
    ISBN 978-1-60060-847-6 (hardcover : alk. paper)
[1. Stories in rhyme. 2. Grandfathers—Fiction. 3. Vegetables—Fiction. 4. Cooking—Fiction.] I. Title.
PZ8.3.F2163Rai 2013          [E]—dc23          2012027279

For Katie

*Stretch, wiggle,*
*sniff, and giggle,*
we scramble from our beds.
Grandpa's making pancakes
for his favorite sleepyheads.

We love to visit Grandpa,
it's always so much fun.
He lets us play outside all day
so we can jump and run.

*Whimper, sigh,*
*cloudy sky,*
is it too wet to play?
We don't want to stay inside
because of rain today.

Grandpa smiles and says to us,
"I know what we can do.
Let's go and find some colors
for my famous Rainbow Stew!"

*Splish, splash,*
*puddle dash,*
we bounce right out the door.
We're off to find some red and green,
some yellow, orange, and more.

Grandpa shows us how to move
between each garden row.
Lifting up the drippy leaves,
we see what colors grow.

Drip, drop,
shake, and hop,
here are lots of greens:
spinach, kale, and cucumbers,
zucchini, peas, and beans.

We find some yellow peppers
and a purple cabbage head.
We tug on rosy radishes
and pop them from their bed.

*Slip, slide,*
*squishy stride,*
we snip off red tomatoes.
We dig into the dark wet dirt
and pull out brown potatoes.

We jump around like grasshoppers and buzz about like bees.

*Pull, pick,*
*gather quick,*
we need more for the stew.
Grab some orange carrots
and a purple eggplant too.

We creep along like ladybugs, and all get muddy knees.

Our basket's full of colors.
We park it by the door.
Our clothes and boots are dripping,
making puddles on the floor.

Grandpa helps us wash our hands
and dries our soggy hair.
"It's almost time to cook," he says,
"so find dry clothes to wear."

*Peel, slice,*
*chop, and dice,*
colors fill the pot.
Stir in herbs and water
and then wait till it gets hot.

Grandpa says he's proud of us,
we're such terrific cooks.
While the stew is heating
we have time to read our books.

*Howl! Yowl!*
*Tummies growl,*
we're a hungry bunch.
It's time to serve up heaping bowls
of Rainbow Stew for lunch.

Yum, yum, yum, yum!

# How to Make Rainbow Stew

You can make your own delicious Rainbow Stew with lots of colorful
vegetables. This recipe makes about 4 cups of stew and takes about
40 minutes to cook. Be sure to have an adult help you.

1 tablespoon olive oil
¼ cup chopped onion
1 garlic clove, minced
¼ teaspoon each of three dried herbs (choose from basil, cilantro,
oregano, parsley, rosemary, and thyme)
½ teaspoon salt and dash of pepper
1 tablespoon water
1 teaspoon cider vinegar
2 cups chopped sturdy vegetables (see choices below)
1 cup liquid (broth, tomato juice, or water)
2 cups chopped tender vegetables (see choices below)

**STURDY VEGETABLES:** bell peppers, broccoli stems, cabbage, carrots, cauliflower, celery,
eggplant, green beans, parsnips, potatoes, turnips, winter squash
**TENDER VEGETABLES:** broccoli tops, kale, peas, spinach, summer squash, tomatoes,
zucchini

1. Heat olive oil in a large pot over low heat. Add onion and stir for 2 minutes.
2. Add garlic and stir for 1 minute.
3. Add herbs, salt, pepper, water, and vinegar. Stir and cook for 1 minute.
4. Add sturdy vegetables. Stir and cook for 2 minutes.
5. Carefully pour in liquid. Stir, cover pot, and cook over low heat for 15 minutes.
6. Add tender vegetables. Stir, cover pot, and cook for 15 minutes. Check occasionally
and stir gently to keep vegetables from sticking to bottom of pot. Add more liquid if
stew starts to stick or gets too thick.
7. Test vegetables for tenderness with a fork. For softer vegetables, cook another
few minutes. Taste and add more salt and pepper, if needed.
8. Ladle stew into serving bowls and *enjoy!*

## OPTIONAL INGREDIENTS

Cook all optional ingredients separately. Add them last and cook stew a few more
minutes until they are heated through. Add more liquid, if needed.

- Barley, lentils, noodles, pasta, rice, or split peas
- Black beans, cannellini beans, garbanzos (chickpeas), or kidney beans
- Beef, chicken, fish, or pork (cut into bite-size pieces)

For more recipes, activities, and fun,
join us at RainbowStewBook.com.